Level 1 is ideal for children who have received some initial reading instruction. Each story is told very simply, using a small number of frequently repeated words.

CW00841344

Special features:

Rose
the fairy
Lily
the fairy
cat
Patch
the elf
6

story words

Rose saw a dog. "We can help that dog," she said.
Lily and Rose went to help the dog.
18
19

Large, clear type

Careful match between story and pictures

Educational Consultant: Geraldine Taylor
Book Banding Consultant: Kate Ruttle

A catalogue record for this book is available from the British Library

Published by Ladybird Books Ltd
80 Strand, London, WC2R 0RL
A Penguin Company

007

ISBN: 978-0-71819-466-6

Printed in China

Fairy Friends

Written by Ronne Randall
Illustrated by Joelle Driedemy

Rose
the fairy
Lily
the fairy

bird
cat
Patch
the elf

Lily was a fairy and
Rose was a fairy, too.

Lily and Rose liked to
help their friends.

Lily saw a bird. “We can help that bird,” she said.

Lily and Rose helped the bird.

Rose saw a cat. "Now we can help that cat," she said.

Lily and Rose helped the cat.

Lily saw a mouse.

"Now we can help that mouse," she said.

It was not a mouse! It was Patch, a bad elf. Patch liked to play tricks.

He had turned into a mouse to trick Lily and Rose.

Rose saw a dog. “We can help that dog,” she said.

Lily and Rose went to help the dog.

It was not a dog. It was Patch the elf! He had turned into a dog to trick Lily and Rose.

"Go away, Patch!" said Lily and Rose. "You are a bad elf!"

Lily saw a fairy. “We can help that fairy,” she said.

“That is not a fairy,” said Rose. “It is Patch. Go away, Patch, you bad elf!”

They saw the fairy, and they saw Patch, too!

"It IS a fairy," said Rose.

"We can help you," said Lily.

Lily and Rose helped the fairy.

Patch turned into a bird and he helped, too.

The fairy was Lily and Rose's new friend.

Now Patch was their friend, too.

How much do you remember about the story of Fairy Friends? Answer these questions and find out!

- What do Lily and Rose like to do?
- Who tricks Lily and Rose?
- Can you remember two of the animals Patch turned into?